A Battleaxe and a Metal Arm 15:

Gallery of Mourning

Samuel Fleming

Copyright © 2022 by Samuel Fleming

Cover Art by David Leahey

ISBN-13: 978-1-954679-41-2 (paperback)
ISBN-13: 978-1-954679-40-5 (ebook)

This one's for my grandfather, and all the others that we've left behind. I know Battleaxe wasn't his cup of tea, but gods bless him, he read every single one.

Contents

"Each death is easier than the
last… What does that say
about us?
—forgotten

Previously...

The heroes crossed the seam at the bottom of the sea, in the ruins of Antrikaumora, and found themselves in a cracked and barren desert. It wasn't long before they heard a commotion in the distance, a lone soul fighting their way through a horde of enemies and a giant condor—

And then the figure headed straight for them. Helesys and Taunauk had been ready for anything, but they relaxed as the figure approached. Shawn had returned to them. Reunited, the three crossed the desert, heading toward a short-lived beacon of light.

The three shared tales of their separation: Helesys telling of their journey beneath the sea, while Shawn told of his new-found powers. While these were a boon, Shawn could not use his power for long, lest he inadvertently drift between realms and be lost again.

Shawn told them of his conversation with the Voice at Meridian—"Only a god can kill another god," it said. When they reached the Wolf King and held his life in their hands, it would have to be Shawn that dealt the killing blow.

He also talked of giving up the life of a god and the life of a mortal—that the truth of his existence puzzled him.

They resolved to continue, fighting through more hordes of zombies, and soon found themselves at the foot of a towering city, one of iron and strange sandstone. One cut from different stone than that of the desert beneath their feet, reminiscent of both the city of Antrikaumora, and somewhere else. Magic steeped and tainted the desert, and they were only just beginning to learn of it.

At the gate of Civirrea they were taken in by a soldier named Chetan, and then the mage named, Zinric. They walked through the streets, seeing commerce and trade—the first true markers of civilization since they'd been trapped in the dungeon. Zinric lead them up one of the towering metal spires, and bid them to rest. It was there, they learned that time moved differently in the dungeon—sometimes faster than the outside world, and other times slower. In Civirrea, they met elves that remembered the single elven city of Novissimé and another that did not.

And as the heroes spoke with the mages, they proposed that the Voice at Meridian might be the Gatekeeper, and that she might be held hostage by the Wolf King.

The mages recognized the heroes as Chosen, and that if they sought passage through the seam of the realm, they would need to prove themselves in the fighting pits. That night, while the heroes talked amongst themselves, Taunauk admitted that his relationship with his father was strained. Shawn dwelled on the contradictory nature of wisp and mortal. Later, Helesys spoke with her wand about its past—that the wand did not think or feel the passage of time as it does now until they were joined together.

The next day, the heroes gathered in the arena—the site where the elders of the city conducted the ritual that brought the Civirrea across the realms. They fought two opponents: The first was a vicious serpent that could teleport across short distances. Even as the creature attacked Helesys, the combined might of the heroes was too much. The second enemy was a molten metal man, seemingly conjured from the same magic as the city. It reached for their weapons nefariously, and Helesys used the holding spell on it. In the shared mindspace, she saw the creature and a mirror of herself—her wand. The metal man was a made-thing, similar to the wand, and it was then that Helesys realized so much of her prowess came from her close bond to the gauntlet and the wand contained inside.

Once the creature was slain, the heroes were escorted back to the towering spire. They learned that Chosen rarely survive the trials, and that the unpromising are weeded out.

They were to be brought before the Angel for judgment before they could pass through the seam. The winding stairwell was reminiscent of the ruins of Antrikaumora, marked with runes and steeped in magic. Helesys recognized the words, though she could not read most of them.

But it was the final words that put her on edge: THE CHOSEN ARE A LIE.

In the final room, they met the Angel, a twisted old-god made of light. Its kind had been imprisoned in the dungeon in ancient times, and they brought Civirrea across the realms. It had seen the ruins of Antrikaumoa and remade the depths beneath the city to contain and focus its own terrible power.

But in its madness, the Angel was loyal to the Wolf King and attacked the heroes with beams of light from its eyes. Helesys used her slow spell to counter the creature. The Angel pushed back against her spell, but Helesys kept her power by channeling all of her might and the beginnings of her inner Rage. Helesys nearly used the Machine of Antrikaumora, but the device had finite power, and she could not risk using it against something other than the Wolf King, itself. Despite their efforts, the creature managed to hit one of the Endroggen spirits, permanently destroying one of Taunauk's ancestors before the Angel finally fell.

When the Angel lay beaten and broken, it cursed them, proclaiming they would never beat the Wolf King—the never-risen sun.

The heroes stepped through the portal and into a pristine castle.

~ ~ ~

What Specters Wait

Helesys, Taunauk, and Shawn stepped through the seam, energy and ether crackling around them. Their feet found stone—though it was not the familiar hall of the dungeon.

The hall they stepped into was clean and bright. Torchlight flickered off of stone that was nearly white. Banners depicting a white wolf's head hung through the hall.

Helesys was struck by a sense of awe and emptiness. They were close to greatness, yet she felt no life in these halls—not even the presence of danger.

Shawn muttered, "I don't like this. Not one bit." He already held a dagger in hand.

Taunauk strode forward without weapons. "I shall go first."

"Right behind you, big guy," Shawn replied uneasily.

Helesys followed, power kindled in body and gauntlet. Whatever lay in store for them, she carried quiet resolve that they would be ready—

That they would win the day.

~

The heroes pressed forward down the immaculate and seemingly unending hall. They stalked in silence, for the deeper they went, the more certain the feeling of mounting dread. It etched in their minds like weather and rain did stone, boring through them, hollowing them.

Helesys kindled power, trying instead to fill herself with determination, but it felt like shoring a candle against a storm. She had seen the things that gods could do; the wonders and horrors wrought across the realms—from across history and space—compressed into the madness that was the dungeon. She had seen more in her short journey across the realms than most others would ever dare to look upon. And she knew that the Wolf King towered above all these.

When one had walked among gods and fought against gods… What words were there for something like the Wolf King? A singularity amongst the world.

Helesys resisted the urge to touch the tiny cube in her pocket, the Machine of Antrikaumora, that supposedly would allow them to stand equal to the God of gods—

To slay *him*.

In those quiet moments of the hall, it felt not just impossible, but absurd.

Yet, they walked forward, bore on by a mix of will, desperation, promise of salvation, or destiny—it did not matter why. It only mattered that they walked forward.

~

Helesys didn't know how long they walked that silent hall, only that they came to a room.

A long red carpet greeted them, covering the stone before it. The Wolf King's banners grew more numerous, masks and statuettes sat atop cherry wood pedestals. As they pressed closer to the room, Shawn reached out to touch one of the statues before pausing midway—thankfully thinking it better not to tempt fate.

Taunauk signaled for them to wait as he peered around the corner. After a moment, he signaled for Helesys to come to the entrance.

"Do you sense any magic? Any traps?" he asked.

Helesys peered around the corner. A plush bedroom stretched out, some hundred feet square, and towered above them. A king's bedroom. Deep red furnishings—wood, linens, and thick cushions, all the color of blood and trimmed in gold and gems—littered the room. Helesys scanned them quickly and found no signs of life therein. Then she opened her senses to magic and found only smoldering remnants.

Her wand answered quietly, as if to reassure her, *There are no traps, Helesys.* Helesys whispered this to her comrades, and the three tentatively stepped into the room.

Shawn muttered, "Do you think this is where… *Tamir above,* he definitely won't be happy that we're in his bedroom. You're sure this is a good idea?"

Helesys crept forward, pushing Shawn's concerns aside.

Of all the things, she walked toward a wide, ornate desk beside a cold fireplace. It was lined with haphazard stacks of parchment and three pens the off-white color of ivory. Most of the sheets were torn or scribbled over so that they were ineligible. She looked to the fireplace and found remnants of scorched pages amongst the ash.

Next there was a magic, shifting globe that showed a different landscape from every angle—the surface showing deep ravines one moment, desert, or ocean the next. But when she turned back to look at an old map, she could not find it again. Each was a fleeting mirage.

There were more sculptures and trinkets, none magical; some of wolves, most were abstract. Jewelry boxes with mundane necklaces and rings. A rack of sashes and robes.

Helesys didn't know what she was searching for, only that nothing *and everything* spoke to her, all at once—everything in the room, covered in the same fine layer of dust.

The bed was immense, far longer and wider than even a giant would need, but low enough for a normal-sized Terran, the crimson covers thrown back, the whole of it covered with a layer of that same fine dust. Helesys peeled back the covers and found that the dust had settled over this haphazard arrangement—it had not been used in some time…

She turned to the paintings lining the wall. Each was a grand landscape: A line of snowy hillside giving way to rolling green; a towering forest; a riverside port at the edge of a city; another that might've been the same city overlooked by a castle. The last was a lake of black, starry sky reflected on its surface. Helesys knew these things were not from the dungeon—she felt this deeply. As she peered into the entrancing landscapes, she found a tiny red figure in each, indescribable and facing away from view.

"He hasn't been here in a long time," Helesys said, only vaguely aware that her allies were close enough to hear. "These are his old things. His old memories. *The old him.*"

"What does that mean?" Shawn asked. "He's still here somewhere, right?"

Helesys nodded with certainty.

Meanwhile, Taunauk stared at the painting—at the rolling green hills. A moment later, he turned. "We should press on."

Taunauk was right, but Helesys couldn't help staring at the room. Her eyes searched it one last time. There had to be something there, something else that might aid them. She thought of rifling through the King's possessions, grabbing anything that spoke to her. Perhaps one of the things might remind him of his old life, might give him pause or muddle him enough for them to gain an edge.

But the weaver shook her head. The man that left these things behind would not be thrown off guard by them. Who knew how long these old things had laid dormant. Forgotten.

Did he even remember the Terran he used to be?

Shawn turned around, frustratedly taking in the sight of the room. "What do we do?"

Taunauk said, "We look for the throne room. Something befitting the king and not the man."

~ ~ ~

Da Coda

The heroes stepped back into the castle hallway, leaving the memories of their enemy behind them. Helesys opened her magic sense and found a distant pull leading them further down the hall. Though Helesys directed them onward, Taunauk led.

They walked for so long that Helesys lost track of time, and the bright stones began to blur together.

Shawn muttered from behind, "Maybe we should stop to rest—where did that come from?"

Where bare stone had been moments before, paintings suddenly appeared. Each was massive, some eight feet tall—nearly tall enough to stretch from floor to ceiling—and stretched some twenty feet across. Others were little bigger than the heroes, each sitting in an ornate frame.

All of them had appeared in a blink.

The three Terrans scanned the halls for signs of life and found none, nor did Helesys feel any sense of danger from her wand.

Shawn added, "What in Movernus's name is going on?"

Neither Helesys nor Taunauk answered. Taunauk walked toward one such painting, entranced by it. Lush green hills stretched across the canvas, so lifelike it seemed as if the grass was blowing in the wind.

Helesys stepped closer to examine the painting and her jaw dropped open. It felt as if she were looking through a window—*she could* see grass blowing in the wind. From that close, she swore she could even feel the heat of the sun.

Beside her, Taunauk's eyes were wide. He reached out a hand to touch the canvas. The painting gave way like water, his fingers disappearing beneath the surface.

Without time to protest, Taunauk stepped through the rippling canvas. Helesys watched as her comrade appeared in the painting as if he'd merely stepped through a portal. He walked along the field, hands trailing over the tops of the long grass.

Helesys reached for the canvas, despite Shawn's protest. "We can't leave him," she said.

Shawn stood, face twisted in hesitation.

Helesys stepped through the painting.

~

She stepped through the canvas and into the lush hills that moments before had been paint. The grass was thick around her, and the sun was warm upon her face—this was intoxicating. For so long, they had wandered the realms in twilight and perpetual dusk. Even the blue skies of the endless sea had been a trick of the light. There had been no sun above them. It tasted of freedom, and there was no sound save for the gentle wind and quietly rolling grass.

Helesys turned and found Shawn had walked through the painting and was taking in the sunlight, too. He looked out over the emerald landscape with a growing smile.

"I can see why it pains you to think of home," Shawn said.

Taunauk stood stoically on the hill. "This is home."

Helesys and Shawn shared an incredulous look.

Shawn said, "Big guy, we're still in the dungeon. This is just a painting or some trick of the mind."

"Shawn's right," Helesys added. "This isn't real."

"It feels real to me," Taunauk replied. Then he started walking down the hill.

Shawn asked, "Where are you going?" He turned and said, "Oh *stercus*."

There was no border to mark the edge of the painting—no way to mark where they had stepped through from the hallway to this realm. Shawn stepped cautiously in that direction, feeling wildly for something—anything. He gave up a moment later and groaned in frustration. There was no way back.

Helesys opened up her senses and felt the subtle pull of magic. "This way," she said, pointing in the direction Taunauk was heading. "We're supposed to go this way."

"Alright, but next time I'm choosing which weird painting we walk into!"

~

Taunauk led them across the green fields in silence. Helesys and Shawn followed a few steps behind.

Shawn said quietly, "I've got to admit, this beats walking through that dreary hallway."

Helesys didn't answer. She was staring off across the fields.

Shawn asked, "Don't you think so?"

She held up a hand to quiet him. "Do you hear that?"

There were voices and a clang of steel. Distant, like the barely audible rumble of a storm. Taunauk sprinted away from them. The others followed.

They stopped two hills away and peered down at a village. Hundreds of tents dotted the green. The people that milled about wore thick furs, and their hair was braided ornately. At the edge of the village, warriors spared with swords and axes.

Helesys's heart swelled as they looked upon an Endroggen village–Taunauk's home. Beside her, her comrade's mouth was agape.

"I never thought I would see this place again," Taunauk said quietly. "It's even more beautiful than in half-remembered dreams." Hesitantly, he stepped down the hill and toward his home.

"*Balach*," said a voice to the right. The three heroes turned and found a giant Endroggen towering over them—appeared as if from the ether. Taunauk's father, Rehkoros.

The three craned their necks to look at him, this warrior that stood nearly twenty feet tall and just as wide.

"*Athair*," Taunauk muttered, "I don't understand."

The immense figure knelt, the impact shook the ground. He wore a patronizing frown. "Where are you going?"

"To see the others. To see my mother."

"We have much more training, Taunauk. The sun has not set."

"I'm not a boy anymore, athair," Taunauk said, his voice tinged with frustration.

Rehkoros laughed and stood, once again towering above them. But the mirth was short-lived. "Ready your axe."

"I want to see my mother," Taunauk said, his voice growing high. He turned to walk past his father and down to the village.

Rehkoros held out his axe to block his path—a mirror of Taunauk's own. It was thick as a felled tree.

"Draw your axe, balach," Rehkoros said again, warmth gone from his voice.

Taunauk stared up at the giant image of his father. Before her eyes, Helesys was no longer looking at her comrade–a young boy stood in his place, no more than ten or eleven. His hair was shorn close. Even gaunt as he was, there was the beginning of a powerful frame.

Axe hanging at his side, Taunauk seethed in a child's voice, "I want to see my mother!"

Rehkoros hoisted his axe and slashed down. Boy Taunauk lunged to the right, narrowly avoiding the crash of his father's axe. The impact spit chunks of earth into the air. Taunauk swung his axe, but his father stepped behind his own blade for safety.

Helesys and Shawn stepped back as Taunauk and Rehkoros fought. They watched, spellbound. There seemed no pretense of sparring in their movements–their attacks were quick and violent, their defenses hurried. Young Taunauk's face twisted into a sneer.

"Should we help him?" Shawn asked.

Helesys barely heard the question. As she stared at the battle, Taunauk seemed both a man and a child with statures to match; his father seemed both a man and a giant–it felt as if she were looking through two windows at once. The weaver's stomach turned and she had to turn away.

Then warning hummed in her wand-arm. As the battle raged between father and son, two other figures walked up the hill toward them. They were both clad in brown robes, and when they were a short distance away, they pulled their hoods. One was a human woman, hair red like fire. She reminded

Helesys fiercely of Perdita, the young channeler from the wode—the made-thing. Helesys could even feel the magic emanating from her. The second figure was a young elven man. His hair was slicked back with sweat, and he had a long dagger held loosely at his side. Menace exuded from both.

Both the red-haired mage and the assassin said in overlapping voices, "You two shouldn't be here. This isn't your place."

Both Helesys and Shawn stood ready. She said, "This is our friend's home. Where he goes, we go."

"Then you will die." The assassin lunged for Shawn, and the rogue backpedaled, their daggers clashing against each other.

The channeler held out her hand and said, "*Ignis flores.*" Fire sprouted from her palm and blotted out Helesys's vision.

The weaver called on her Ring of Winter, and felt the familiar and painful pull of the cold tendril along her nerves, shouting, "*Hieme Murum!*" The shield of frost surrounded her, and the fire coursed harmlessly around the shell.

Helesys let the icy shield waver, and lunged forward with the Gar of Shéslang. Though the red-haired mage had no weapons of her own, she twisted and dodged from Helesys's attacks.

"*Greim oirre,*" she said. Vines shot from the ground, snaring around Helesys's ankles and then her arms. Even with bolstered strength, she could not wrench free. The vines dragged her down, trying to pull Helesys to her knees.

The weaver grit her teeth and called upon her *frost shield* again, the icy swirling and thickening at her command. She felt the vines grow still, and Helesys uttered the words, "*Frigus inspiratione.*"

The swirling vortex exploded outward, sending shards of frozen vines at her attacker. The red-haired channeler screamed, and when the air cleared, she lay mangled on the ground.

The gasping channeler raised a hand up to the sky. Gray clouds rolled toward them from across the hills. She began to mutter the old words–

And was cut short by Helesys's blast. The weaver turned away from the charred remains of the channeler.

Across the hills, the battles still raged. Shawn and the assassin were a blur of flesh and steel. Despite the fury, he was still Terran. He hadn't discarded his wrappings and become ethereal. Meanwhile, Taunauk still fought his father, his cries and frustration growing louder–still that shadow of a boy. As Helesys saw this, she realized that these creatures were not just denizens of the dungeon–they were something more.

"*Lente et gravis*," Helesys said, hexing both the assassin and the giant.

As soon as she spoke, the assassin turned and sprinted toward her, teeth bared in a snarl. Even hexed, he was inhumanly quick. He was nearly upon her when his eyes grew wide and he fell to the ground–Shawn perched overtop him, daggers buried in the thing's back.

Across the field, a giant groaned. Young Taunauk cleaved into the giant's knee, felling him and shaking the ground. Slashes flew across the creature's sword arm and then desperate hand. The creature bellowed, "Enough bala–" before it was cut short by the boy's axe cleaving through his head.

Taunauk stood beside the felled giant that wore his father's face, and he screamed. Agony echoed over the green fields, and none of the villagers in the valley so much as turned to look. It was as if they were ghosts, or merely a painting.

~

Silence hung over the hills for a long time before Taunauk walked over to them. He no longer looked anything like the boy he had been. He was the towering barbarian she had come to know, and weary now. His gait was unsteady, and splatters of blood covered his front.

"Are you alright?" Helesys asked.

"No," Taunauk replied.

Before he could answer, the sky grew dark. Storm clouds were still rolling in, turned red by the setting sun. In the valley below, Endroggen retreated inside their tents.

Whatever Taunauk had been about to say was quickly forgotten as he turned and walked to the valley below. "Come," he said.

Helesys and Shawn followed, leaving the bodies of the fallen behind.

As they approached the village, Helesys opened her senses to danger and magic, yet found none. Despite this, she kept power kindled.

Taunauk led them to a tent no different from the others. He opened it and all three stepped through. However big the tent had seemed at first, it was now two or three times taller from inside. Two bedrolls lay side by side on the canvas flooring. Taunauk sat cross-legged on one, suddenly looking like a young boy again. Even though Helesys and Shawn looked unchanged, their statures were the same as young Taunauk.

A boy lay on the other bedroll, long braided hair laying in a heap beside him—a contrast to Taunauk's stubble. The boy picked his teeth with a shard of bone.

"Don't be such a lollywort," the boy said. "Your father will forgive you." He chuckled. "He should be proud of you. You're supposed to be a great fighter."

Young Taunauk replied, "It doesn't feel like a victory."

"Bah."

"What do you know, Thuldreth? You still spare with knee-highs," Taunauk jested.

Thuldreth chuckled. "And I'm better than every single one of them!"

For a moment, the air grew light as the boys laughed, and Helesys knew she was witnessing something fleeting in young Taunauk's life. Though the boy laughed, the image alternated with the Taunauk she knew. Quiet tears ran down his face.

The image in the tent changed again. Taunauk and Thuldreth were young men, and now the contrast couldn't be more stark. Taunauk still sat stoically, hair shorn to stubble, while Thuldreth lounged lightheartedly.

Thuldreth rose suddenly, excitement on his face. "I've been sworn to secrecy, but I can't stay silent, Taunauk. Cil and I confessed our love to each other. We will be joined under the next full moon."

Silence hung between them, and young Taunauk's face twisted into a smile. "That's good, Thuldreth. That's good," he said, as if trying to convince himself.

Thuldreth's happiness waned at this. "You know, she speaks of you often. She says that even though we're to be joined, I will always be your shield brother. And you will always be a part of our family."

At this, young Taunauk looked down at the canvas between them.

Thuldreth's face sullened. "I am sorry—"

"Do not be. You are not confined by my burden."

"I am still sorry. I am not blind. I know your burden, and I do not revel in your hardships."

Taunauk said, "No one knows that better than I. I can still be happy for my shield brother."

"Your face says otherwise."

Taunauk's eyes fell to the canvas floor between them. "I can be both happy and sad. I am Endroggen, same as you."

"Of course. I meant nothing by it."

Taunauk continued, "One day, when my task is complete, I will have a family of my own."

"Will you?"

"Yes."

Thuldreth's voice was weary. "Have the elders confided in you yet?"

"They do not need to. When the time is right, they will tell me what is needed."

"There is talk," Thuldreth whispered. "I heard that—"

Taunauk held up a hand to quiet his shield brother. "You forget yourself, brother. It is not my place to know. I am *aonar*. Besides, I know what they say of me. I am alone—I am not deaf."

Thuldreth waved dismissively. "They are *sgudal*. They haven't the strength—"

"*Enough*, Thuldreth." Young Taunauk lay on his cot and turned away. Shortly after, his shield brother reluctantly did the same.

~

Both the memory and the tent faded from view, leaving the heroes standing in the middle of a slumbering Endroggen village.

Helesys and Shawn looked at their comrade. Taunauk stood before them, head hung low. In that moment, he looked more weary than ever, as if he'd fought across the uncountable realms without rest.

"In those days I had much to be angry about," he said. "I spent my childhood training with my father, the elders, and with Thuldreth, my shield brother. Though I lived with my tribe, I wasn't permitted to be a part of it. I was to be aonar in all ways. I do not remember my mother nor my other siblings. My shield brother was my only… My only tether to the world.

"We had both thought that my journey would be close at hand… He could not have known how much I would have to wait for the call."

In the span of a breath, the sun rose on the Endroggen plains. Villagers appeared suddenly and mulled around the heroes. The three were specters amongst the people.

Thuldreth and a young woman walked by, baby swaddled across her chest. He kissed her forehead while the infant cooed.

A moment later, the village receded, and again the three heroes stood on the surrounding hill, peering down. Helesys could just make out the two figures of Thuldreth and his lover.

Beside her, she saw Taunauk both as her comrade and as a young man. He had paused his sword training. His face was hard, and no wrinkles lined it. Both images of him fixated on the couple and the village.

"I waited eight more years," Taunauk said. "I watched his boy, Sunder, grow… When the elders finally confessed my task, when they told me of the lost souls of Accaelum, I left in the dead of morning. I did not say goodbye.

"I am both grateful to have him as a brother, and angry that he abandoned me. That is the way of the Endroggen: We must both feel and not feel our emotions; suffer them and bury them for later. Just as my people needed me and also spurned me. The barbarian life is one of duality. I must honor a village I was not a part of. I must save the souls of Endroggen I have never known."

Taunauk turned to his comrades defiantly. Quiet rage smoldered in his eyes, and Helesys knew he was speaking as much to his father and the other souls as he spoke to her and Shawn. "I will do these things because my people require it. Because I am the only one that can. I am the vessel of the lost souls of Accaelum. We will win our freedom."

~ ~ ~

Diminuendo

Lush green fields and warm sun gave way to harsh stone and cool air as the three heroes found themselves suddenly back in the castle hallway.

Shawn muttered, "What was all that about?"

"They were memories," Taunauk replied.

"No, I mean before those. What was with the Terrans—the creatures—we fought?"

Taunauk said, "That was a memory too." When his comrades looked at him, he added, "At first, it was a memory. That day, I grew tired of training. I wanted to see my mother. My father refused. In my rage, I wounded him that day. Nothing more than a cut upon his shoulder, but it felt as if I had cleaved a gorge between us… It was easier when I didn't remember my life."

Helesys asked, "Why did you go into the painting?"

Taunauk shrugged meekly. "I have a dozen Endroggen souls in my head, all wanting to see home again. It was hard to refuse."

After a moment, Helesys said, "Let's keep moving. The seam is down the hall."

Taunauk led them. Again, they passed tapestries laden with the familiar wolf's head visage. And again they found an enormous painting.

The canvas stretched out, a swirl of white, silver, and blue. Snow-dusted mountain peaks jutted through the clouds, and in the center of it all, a waterfall—the water rising from the river, up the rocks and into the abyss of sky.

Shawn stepped forward, entranced by the painting. He reached out a timid, shaking hand, but did not touch it.

"What is it?" Helesys asked.

Shawn whispered, "The mountains of Eluthiya—the gate of the realm of dreams. *I remember.*" Shawn turned to Helesys and Taunauk, voice straining with excitement. "Come. You have to see it for yourself." Shawn stepped through the painting, and his cloak blew in the wind.

Breath caught in her throat as Helesys watched her comrade. It wasn't until Taunauk stepped forward into the painting that Helesys brought herself to follow.

~

Helesys stepped through the painting and felt the swirling, humid wind of the mountaintops tug at her cloak and her hair. The clouds obscured much, save for the strange sight of the waterfall rising into the pale sky.

Despite the fog, Helesys was overcome with emotion and awe. The concerns of before—of struggle and strife—felt as far away as the bottom of the mountain. She wasn't just standing on the precipice of the mountain; she was on the precipice of freedom and wonder.

She looked at Taunauk and found his lips parted in a similar smile. It was the most she had ever seen on her measured comrade.

In front of them, Shawn stood in front of the waterfall, arms held out in welcome. He called over the rocks, "Come, and I'll show you how to fly!"

Neither weaver nor barbarian could resist jogging over to their comrade.

Shawn said, "We are going up the waterfall—the *Dream Bridge*. To fly, you need to let go. That's it, just let go."

"Let go of what?" Helesys asked.

"Everything. Don't think about who you are, why we're here, or anything else. Focus on the mist and the wind. Don't even think about your body or your feet when they leave the ground. Just the mist and the wind." As Shawn said this, he began to float. "Trust me."

Helesys tried. She thought of the mist and the wind, the sensations of them on her skin. And as she did, her mind wandered. She thought of home, the halls of Great House Byyra… They had never felt further away. Her family, her people, the Eternal War, all of it was… muted. Even the dungeon and the realms they'd traveled through—the memories were hazy. What were those things compared to true freedom?

Shawn's voice, "What's wrong, Taunauk?"

Helesys opened her eyes and found herself floating beside Shawn. Her heart swelled with excitement, but even this felt muted and distant. Of course she was flying—why wouldn't she be?

But Taunauk was still on the rocks. He stared up at them stoically. "I can't."

"Of course you can," Shawn replied. "Just let go."

Taunauk shook his head. "Everything I've done, everything I am, is for my people. I cannot forget them, or my home."

The soft rush of water hung in the air between them.

"Go," Taunauk finally said. "I will find you after. Search your memories, as I did, but do not forget why we are here. And where we must go. Do not forget our task." There was a wistfulness in his eyes. Things unspoken.

Shawn replied, "We won't forget."

Helesys didn't reply. She felt sadness for her comrade. For her friend. But even this was faint and soon forgotten.

She and Shawn were already rising into the clouds.

~

Helesys and Shawn soared into the sky. Wind and mist billowed around her, and Helesys lost all sight of the world beneath.

To call it *flying* didn't do the sensation justice. Birds flew. The air the two heroes moved through was thick with clouds, but not wet. It was air—

But it was also water, for Helesys felt the sluggish sensation of swimming—

But nor was it *swimming*. Fish swam.

Helesys's mind struggled to comprehend the sensation: This strange movement that was neither flying, swimming, falling or floating...

"Don't think too hard about it," Shawn said. She had nearly forgotten about him. Shawn flew beside her, his form nearly indistinguishable from the silvery clouds. "It's like trying to remember the start of a dream, or that moment you fell asleep. It's ephemeral." He smiled coyly. "The closest thing I can think to describe it is *dreamsurfing*."

Helesys dwelled on this. Soft currents swirled against her skin. They did not pull her, nor force her. It was the gentlest urging, the faintest whisper of suggestion.

She asked, "Where are we going?"

"Anywhere we want."

Images began to appear in the mist. A cobblestone path overlooking farmland of endless golden wheat. The stones of the path grew large, swelling to giant boulders that lined a frozen coast while titanic waves battered them. A family of elves walked the distant shore. As Helesys moved closer, the child aged, growing until she was a young woman. The scene changed and the young elf stood in a glistening ballroom, hands clasped to her mouth and answering a breathless *yes* to her lover's marriage proposal. Then glistening chandeliers grew large, turning into towering cave formations. Torchlight flickered in the darkness, and Helesys watched a young wizard reach for a long forgotten sword smoldering with magic. With a gust of wind, the torchlight faded, and Helesys and Shawn were threading the treetops of a dark forest.

Though it was Helesys and Shawn that surfed, it felt as if the images passed by like specters.

"What is all this?" Helesys asked. "Are these memories?"

"What does it matter?"

"In Taunauk's painting, he saw memories. Are these yours?"

"No," Shawn said, "not mine, and they're not really memories. Though, I suppose most people dream of places they've been or things they've done or wished they'd done differently. These are dreams, Helesys. Some might've been mine, but I couldn't remember. All dreams pass through here."

"Why are we here?"

The wisp looked taken aback by the question. "Why wouldn't we be here? This is my home."

"But it's not. This is just a trick of the dungeon, Shawn."

"That's not my name. My name is Soldei Milent." As Shawn spoke, his voice seemed to echo all around her, as if he was fading into the mist, becoming as incomprehensible as the spaces around them.

"And who have you been for the past dozen realms, Soldei? Your name has been Shawn. You forget your way and your purpose."

"I haven't forgotten," Shawn replied. "I know what's at stake even better than you do. Would you like to see the Wolf King? I can find him right now… All I have to do is surf to him—"

"No!" Helesys shouted. She reached out with a translucent hand, and even though it looked as if she fumbled blindly into the mist, she felt a form beneath her metal hand—thin and spindly, barely solid.

"We cannot risk it," she said, wrenching Shawn's ghostly form from the mist. "You must stop this at once!"

Shawn struggled, and the two of them spun haphazardly through the mist, then tumbled over one another. There was no sensation of up nor down, only the whirling trails of silver and white that followed them.

"Let go of me, you *thing!*" Shawn seethed. She felt cold and wet hands prying at her grasp. A moment later, Shawn wrenched himself free.

Suddenly, Helesys was motionless in the mist.

And alone.

"Shawn… Soldei Milent!" she called.

There was no answer.

~

Helesys wandered the mist. She neither walked nor flew, for she had no body with which to do so. Nor did she have any sensation of moving at all; the mist swirled absently, as if she were completely still.

She called for Shawn until her voice was hoarse. Finally, she fell silent.

A world came to her, unbidden, as if it had always been there, and the veil of mist only lifted to reveal it.

She stood upon a cobblestone path, looking out over fields of wheat. Again, she felt the stones beneath begin to change and grow—

Helesys refused. Instead of letting her mind wander or surf, she willed herself to stay there. Gradually, the mist receded more and more, revealing rolling hills and a village in the distance.

Without knowing why, she strode across the fields, refusing for her feet to leave the ground. She was afraid to think on the urge too much, afraid that an errant thought might pull her to another scene. The longer she walked, the more the mist receded, revealing sprawling fields all around her. The village didn't just grow in the distance, it also seemed to change—a factory grew large and fat like a tick, swelling with metal and smoke, and belching the latter into the sky.

Helesys stopped in the middle of the field—suddenly aware that she was not alone.

A figure stood to her right, clad in a long pale robe that shielded the whole of it. Like a blemish in the wheat. A knot formed in Helesys's throat, one that preceded even the hum of warning in her gauntlet. For a moment, she feared it was the Wolf King, but quickly pushed that particular fear aside. Nor was it the Gatekeeper—*it* was something else. Tension hung in the silence. Some moments later, Helesys realized that the *thing's* robe was not made of cloth or fur—it was made of pale white skin, thick with folds and riddled with thin green veins.

And that was not the most unsettling part of *it*.

Helesys was trapped in the castle—in the dungeon. This painting was some other realm, small and specialized. Perhaps it was a mirrored of some kind, reflecting Shawn's memories, just as the other painting had been Taunauk's memories.

Her earlier intuition wasn't right: This *thing* wasn't part of the painting. It wasn't a blemish on the wheat. It was a stain—a hole in the canvas, itself.

She kindled power, for the little good she feared it would do.

"What are you?" Helesys asked.

"I am somewhere between void and life, between joy and sorrow, between unending and infinitesimal." Its voice was breathy like a whisper born upon the wind, and the mist shuddered at the sound. "I am *everything* you think I am, Helesys Byyra."

The whisper of her name made the weaver's skin crawl. In spite of her fear, she had to ask:

"Are you the Voice? The one that's been helping us?"

"No."

Helesys swallowed, and asked the question to which she already knew the answer. "You're not here, are you?"

"I am, and I am not."

"What I mean is… You're not trapped here in the dungeon."

"No. I am born of dreams, and dreams cannot be bound. I go where I please."

"Then why are you here?" Helesys asked, her voice barely a whisper.

It came closer, stopping six feet from her. Whether *it* walked or floated, she could not tell. She was only thankful that *it* stopped.

"I came for you and for Soldei Milent. It's been too long since he escaped to the mortal realm, but now I think I'll leave him here to rot."

"Are you Tamir?" she asked. "Shawn—Soldei's father?"

It laughed quietly, and its faint breath made the realm shudder. She already knew *it* wasn't Tamir.

"Then what do you want with me?" she asked. Helesys dredged power, if only to still her quaking voice.

"Soldei Milent keeps strange company—most strange, Helesys Byyra. I merely want to keep an eye on you.

For a flicker of a moment, it was as if the hood of the *thing* had been pulled back, revealing a void. Before Helesys could blink, she was back in the field, staring at the skin-robe of the creature.

Then the creature vanished, leaving Helesys alone in the field.

~

Helesys resolved not to linger any longer in the field or in the realm. She moved as fast as possible across the fields, crossing them in a breath, and arrived in the village. Even from the edge, she could already smell the iron and sulfur, and hear the clangs of metal from the factory.

Again, she was struck by the eerie feeling of neither walking nor flying—now more apparent than ever as the stones passed silently beneath her.

She was drawn to the factory and let herself go there. Iron walls rose far higher than any of the quaint dwellings of the rest of the village. There was a steady stream of young men and women, and some elves that filed through the main door. As Helesys drew near, she found a space in the line of Terrans and fell in with them, drifting into the factory.

Her eyes adjusted to the sweltering darkness. Metal loomed all around her, the factory towering so high that the everlit candles above looked like stars. Though candles hovered closer, they were blotted out by the molten slag that flowed all around—falling in streams from floors above and pooling in vats and cauldrons littering the floor. All around the steady clangs of smithing hammers rang out—but these were too deep and resonant to be made by Terrans; they sounded of giants and things not of this world.

Helesys felt a pull, leading her somewhere in the maelstrom of heat and echoing metal. She found him moments later, a young man hunched over a pool of slag. Thin, bandaged arms worked a crank. Sweat beaded on his face. There was nothing remarkable about him, save for his tattoos and his ears—one human, the other elven.

"Shawn," Helesys whispered, reaching out a tentative hand.

Shawn recoiled. "Who—Helesys! I'm not—I'm not dreaming." He stood and grasped her by the shoulders, then embraced her. "By Tamir, I thought I'd lost you."

"I'm here," she said, slowly relaxing, hoping that Shawn had come to his senses. "What happened?"

He pulled away reluctantly. "I lost myself, I think. The realm of dreams is… *intoxicating*. I'm sorry."

"Think nothing of it, but Shawn, we can't stay here. We need to get out of here. Back to Taunauk and out of the painting."

Shawn's eyes wavered as if he'd forgotten, but then the rogue nodded. "I think I have to go home."

~

Shawn led Helesys through the maze of the factory and out into the street. As they walked, mist pressed in around them from all sides until there was nothing left, save for the next couple stones in front of them.

Helesys asked, "Do you know the way?"

Shawn nodded. "Don't worry. It's come back to me. It's easier to remember when I'm mortal."

She looked at him, considering his thin and weary figure. He looked so very tired, so much more than his age would suggest.

"There's something else…" she said. As they walked, she told him of her run in with the creature that wore the pale skin-cloak. And as she did, she watched her comrade's eyes grow wide and then wider still.

When Helesys told him that the creature was interested in her, Shawn stopped on the stones and stared at her.

At the end, she asked, "What is it?"

"*It* is the enemy of my father." Tamir, the god of dreams.

"So it's the god of nightmares?"

Shawn smirked and insisted they keep walking. For a moment, he debated with himself. "Even if I could remember their entire history, it wouldn't matter. Do you remember the stories that Movernus made the world?" Helesys nodded, and he continued. "Well, ours is not the only *world*, our time is not the only *when*. It's very similar to the dungeon, in a way."

"Multiple realms, multiple worlds."

"Yes. The creature is from another world. Some wisps say that *it* is from one of the oldest worlds, born from a time before dreams and reality were separate. *Its* name is Nimicus."

Helesys shook her head. "Then what is *it* doing here? What kind of creature can come and go from a place like this, one where even spirits and gods cannot escape?"

"Something looking for you, apparently."

"I'm serious, Shawn."

"So am I." The rogue paused again on the cobblestone path. "You don't understand. Nimicus doesn't idly take notice of people. *It* always has an agenda—not that its agenda is something that can be explained or understood. There is no way I could even begin to explain how dangerous it is, though I suppose it showing up here of all places is testament enough."

Helesys asked, "Okay, so what do we do?"

"Nothing. If Nimicus—its power here must be limited. That's why it came to you and hid from me." Shawn rubbed the stubble on his face idly. "First, we have to worry about escaping and beating the Wolf King. Then we can worry about Nimicus. What's wrong?"

Helesys had tried not to let the concern show on her face, but Shawn had read it plainly. "Why doesn't the god of dreams take care of *it*?"

Shawn said plainly, "Tamir is dead. He couldn't defeat Nimicus, so Tamir cut himself into a thousand pieces—each of us a wisp. Myself and the others are what remain of the god of dreams."

"Even a thousand of you can't defeat it…"

Shawn shook his head. "That's not it at all. Tamir made a thousand of us so that we could flee. So those shards of him might survive a while longer."

The realization hung heavy in the air and settled silently between them. It wasn't until they started walking again that Shawn spoke.

"Nimicus did me one favor though, merely speaking of *it* brought a bunch of bad memories. Memories, nonetheless."

~

They walked down the cobblestone streets until they came to a squalid dwelling. The mist faded, revealing a slum street lined with ramshackle homes, so haphazard in their construction that one couldn't tell where one house ended and another began. Soot from the factory settled like fine snow across the scene.

Shawn sighed and stared at one crooked door. "This is it. This is home." After a moment, he pushed it open. The hinges groaned.

The bottom of the door brushed aside soot that had worked its way through the threshold, and more of the powder settled in the nooks and crannies of the dwelling. A grandfather and granddaughter sat on one of the three cots, reading to each other. Soot highlighted his wrinkles and powdered her face.

The girl looked up at the pair of them, smile widening. "Shawn!"

She sprung from the cot and lunged for him. Shawn knelt and spread his arms.

A second Shawn appeared, for a moment only a ghostly visage. He scooped the girl up in his arms and spun around, sharing her smile and laughter. Then they sat together, the three of them on one cot and read to one another.

Meanwhile, the real Shawn hadn't stood. He was still kneeling and silently watching the scene unfold. As the three took turns reading to one another, their words grew faint.

Shawn scooched over to the wall opposite of the three, wiped his eyes, then patted the ground beside him. Helesys smiled and sat down with him.

"Are you alright?" She asked.

He nodded. "I will be. Being a wisp was intoxicating. It was true freedom. But coalescing and becoming mortal made things just feel so much more real. Even this place, even the long tedious hours of the factory, felt so much more real than surfing dreams ever was.

"But it was hard—gods, it was hard to live as a mortal. To stay and work and eat and shit… to feel tired and hungry… even just coming home every day to the two of them. It was so hard, Helesys, to give up the freedom of being a wisp.

"That's why I left them. It was too much, so I left. I forgot what I was and how to become a wisp again, so I left to find a way. I think that's why—yeah—I sought out this place. I think I thought that the dungeon held the answers. That's why I'm here." Shawn fell silent a moment, face curling with emotion.

Helesys put a reassuring hand on his shoulder. "We'll get out of here. I swear it."

"It's not that," he said quietly. "I wasn't happy as a god, wasn't happy as a mortal. What does that mean, Helesys? Am I doomed to waver between the two, never finding my place?"

Both fell silent while the memory played on silently before them.

Finally, Helesys said, "Perhaps it is about finding a balance. Do not stay too long as one or the other, that way you can appreciate both, and you do not forget your blessings. Perhaps that is the key to satisfying both halves of yourself."

Shawn nodded slowly. "Perhaps."

"What about Nimicus? Was he—*it*—a part of why you became mortal?"

"No. Though if *it* ever came after me, I think some time as a mortal would throw *it* off my trail."

"Good," she said, then added, "We should find Taunauk. Something tells me we're not quite finished in this realm."

"Can I have just a few more minutes?"

Helesys smiled meekly. "Of course." They sat together and watched the muted scene.

She mused that it was in those quiet moments—Taunauk and his shield brother, Shawn and the family, even Helesys and her comrades—where they found their truths. For all the power they'd reveled in, all the terrible things they'd overcome, all the wondrous things they'd seen, it was those quiet moments that they were trying to get back. Those quiet moments they didn't want to let go of.

~ ~ ~

Volta

Shawn led Helesys out of the tiny house and across the soot-lined cobblestones. From there they walked a forest and climbed jagged mountain peaks to find the waterfall that marked the *Dream Bridge*. The entire journey passed in the same blur that accompanied surfing. Helesys couldn't tell whether hours or mere moments had passed—

She only knew that once again she stood in the white stone hallway, staring at the painting of mist.

"That was quick," Taunauk said. The barbarian was standing beside them, wearing a look of surprise.

Helesys and Shawn shared a glance.

Shawn shrugged and turned. "I guess it wasn't a lot to see."

Taunauk didn't look as if he believed the rogue. "I hope you found part of what you were looking for."

"I did. Thanks. I'll… I'll tell you about it later. Let's just keep moving."

Taunauk grunted in affirmation, then led them further down the hall. Helesys looked at the rogue, but he wouldn't meet her eyes.

They walked in silence for some time before they came to the next painting. It was enormous, like the others before. It depicted a mountain range, and a sprawling city of glass and metal spires. The elven city of Novissimé was so large it bridged two peaks.

Helesys realized it was Novissimé, but it was a moment before she realized it was *home*. Her heart was heavy in her chest, her legs doubly so.

Shawn said, "That's it, isn't it? Your city."

Taunauk laid a heavy hand on her shoulder. "We're right behind you. Go when you're ready."

Helesys nodded, took another breath, and stepped through the painting.

~

Helesys stepped through the painting and into a grand hallway. The whole of it was frosted glass, cut seamlessly by magic some centuries ago. It would've been impossible to tell from the other glass spires if it weren't for the twisting serpents of House Byyra etched into the walls.

Emotions swirled in Helesys, but she didn't have time to know how to feel.

Two elven children ran past, both in bright green dresses. Long white hair and long dark hair trailing behind them.

"Come on, Helesys," young Aradi said. "Your studies can wait!" She reached for her sister's hand, but young Helesys pulled away.

"I can't," young Helesys said. "You don't get it."

"What's so important about your schooling that you have to do it *now*?"

Little Helesys sighed. "One day I'll be the head of the family, and I'll have to take over all the things that mom and dad do. I have to study. Mom said."

Young Aradi groaned. "You're just a sourshard."

"Are not!"

"Are too." Aradi took off down the hall, young Helesys chasing her heels.

But little Helesys only followed until the end of the hall before she turned to go toward her studies.

Behind her, Shawn asked, "Were you always such a sourshard?"

Helesys smirked. "I guess I was. Aradi used to joke that I was born an old elf. I guess she was right. It's… hard to remember, sometimes."

Helesys walked the hall, tracing the path that her younger self had gone. There was an open room without a door, lined with several small desks and a lectern. These were made of dark wood—such natural finery was hard to come by in a city of stone, metal, and glass. Young Helesys sat at one of the desks alone, while one of her tutors stood at the front.

Professor Dallan was there currently. She was short and pointed with her movements—like an attentive bird. She gestured repeatedly to several mathematical drawings on the stoneboard. Or were they alchemical drawings? Helesys stood in the entryway of the small room, and should've been able to see the short distance, but the stoneboard was blurry. Helesys instead tried to listen to her old tutor, but the elf's voice was muted and indistinct.

Shawn asked, "What's she teaching you about?"

Helesys turned, frustration growing inside her. "I don't remember."

Shawn looked as if he was going to ask another question but hesitated. Beside him, Taunauk watched the scene with interest.

Helesys turned back to the classroom. "I should remember. I spent most of my early life in this room. My parents hired all the brightest minds in Novissimé to tutor me. They wanted nothing but the best for the child that was going to take over the House.

Aradi should've been there, but she skipped many school days, preferring to spend her time doing just about anything else. Some days she wandered the merchants' quarters, taking in the sights of alchemical shelves, metallurgy troves, and stalls of fruits and elixirs. Aradi was gifted; somehow she always kept up, despite her truancy.

It was a stark contrast between the sisters—one sister who seemingly wanted nothing of their House, and Helesys, who always felt that she wasn't doing enough.

The classroom in front of them shifted and changed. A breath later, and Helesys was staring at her mother's study. Wynbella stood behind her desk, which despite its size was only a fraction of as imposing as her mother was. Helesys stood across the room, only slightly younger than she looked now. Somehow, she was fearless in the face of it.

"I am going to join the legion," past Helesys said.

"Absolutely not. Your father forbade it, and I am standing beside his words."

"I don't need your permission anymore."

Though the words were said plainly and without vitriol, Helesys winced. They felt so strange coming from her mouth.

Wynbella drew herself up proudly. "It's not a matter of permission. What if something should happen to you out there? You would spit on your father's memory."

Past Helesys said, "You speak as if Aradi is dead. She would take care of things."

"Your sister—she never cared about the House or about her studies. She would sooner flee Novissimé."

Past Helesys breathed deep. "Mother, I'm joining the legion."

"Why?"

"What do you mean?"

Wynbella slumped into her chair and suddenly looked tiny behind the desk. "It's a simple question. Why is joining the legion more important to you than taking care of your family's legacy?"

"I care about both. I'm a talented spellweaver; I could help the legion."

"It's too dangerous."

Past Helesys stood firm. "There hasn't been a casualty recorded in ten years."

"And do you know why that is? Because the legion and their simulacrums hold the front. That *casualty* ten years ago wasn't just one elf—it was six. Six officers on the Harbor of Rori. All because they foolishly thought they could push the eternal front forward."

"I know the history, mother." The first hints of aggravation slipped through Past Helesys's voice—

While dejection shown on Wynbella's face. "You're too young to understand how futile it is. Pushing forward risks mages that we cannot spare. It is only because of the simulacrums that we hold the line against the Shadowkind."

"All the while, their shadows grow more numerous. We cannot continue on another millenia while pretending that—"

"Enough." Wynbella rubbed her temples. "I can't... I can't do this anymore. If I can't change your mind, then get out of my sight."

Helesys watched the echo of herself leave the room, and then the memory finally faded. The heroes stood alone in an empty hallway of frosted glass.

Helesys's shoulders felt heavy. It was not the first argument she'd had with her mother, nor the last. But she would give much to forget all of them.

~

The heroes lingered motionless in the empty hall.

Taunauk broke the silence. "What happened to your father?"

Helesys smiled bitterly to herself. "They say that elves are ageless, but that's not true. We just don't grow old the same way that humans do. We don't show it as much. My people live for a few hundred years. Some live for a thousand. Rarely do any live longer.

"Illness comes on suddenly and gravely, usually while we're sleeping. Some elves even worship Tamir as the God of the End..." Helesys cleared her throat. "My father died in his sleep. It was his time, and it pained my mother dearly. I think that was why she was so afraid to let me go."

The frosted glass of the hallway splintered and shattered. It fell like an avalanche, revealing a black mountain slope. The powdered glass vanished in the wind. Helesys, Taunauk, and Shawn stood on the top of the black mountain, overlooking a strange world—a battlefield.

The largest front of the war was contained to the twisted landscape between twin mountain ranges. Their peaks bled an aurora of pink and red into the gray sky, like claws tearing open a wound.

From where they stood, the scene was writ large. The simulacra armies of the elves flowed across the hills like glistening snow. Each officer commanded hundreds, sometimes even thousands, of the soulless, magical creations. They followed orders without pause or consideration for their own safety, throwing themselves headlong into the dark armies of the shadowkind, which pooled like tar across the landscape. There, on the eternal battlefield, the armies of soulless creations were locked in endless struggle—light and dark, unflinching, unyielding. An entire horizon filled with war.

Every minute or two, a spark of lightning or blast of fire would illuminate the battlefield—a dozen mages working in unison to concentrate and magnify their magic into artillery. That was the great irony: It took concentrated magic to hurt the shadowkind—a single mage's power was not enough. So, the elves called upon their soulless constructs—both simulacra and artillery batteries—to fight the soulless shadowkind.

The memories came back to her, trickling like the armies across the landscape of the landscape. She had seen the immensity of the Eternal War. She was no stranger to it, but seeing it from such a height—seeing the true scale of it— sapped the air from her chest.

She was only vaguely aware that her allies stepped next to her, taking in the sight with the same tentative breaths as she.

"This is the war?" Taunauk asked.

"Part of it," she replied. "There are smaller fronts, but this is the Maw. This is where it all started.

"You can't see it from up here, but in the middle of the swarm of shadows is the Ruins of Inium. Long ago, my people sought a pocket realm where they could practice warfare and test weapons without blighting the world. So they opened a seam to this place. It was supposed to be barren and uninhabited. Somewhere down there underneath the swarm of black is that fateful place where the first seam was struck."

"Movernus…" Shawn muttered. "Why don't you just close it?"

Helesys smiled grimly. "They tried. The shadowkind followed them. Thankfully, their numbers were few, and the elves pushed them back. Now they keep three breaches open perpetually.

"For as numerous and impressive as the shadowkind are, they are simple creatures—like made-things. They throw themselves futilely at the elves' simulacra without thought of tactics or fear of pain or death. And they do not open seams of their own while they can sense other seams—no matter how far behind our lines they are.

"So it has been, and so it will be. We cannot retreat for fear that they will find a way into our world, nor can we advance, for their strength grows in tandem with ours."

Taunauk said quietly, "You have made a world of ruin."

Helesys could not disagree.

~

The scene of the shadowrealm changed around the heroes, shrinking from a grand overlook to the narrow confines of the Passage of Sanhara, a canyon on the outskirts of the steppes of the Maw. The walls of the canyon were striped in grays and blacks, an otherworldly geological strata. But stranger than the look of the place was the feel and the smell—the air of the shadowrealm was impossibly thin, and the only reason elves survived here at all was due to the realm's latent magic. The elves simply did not need to breathe while they fought. This also had the strange side effect that the sensation of temperature was intermittent and fleeting—a chill breeze that disappeared in a blink. The smell of metal and chemical lingered faintly in the air, bringing with it the thought of blood and embalming fluid.

It was a horrid place—something alien that strained the mind and the senses. Even having served time there on the battlefield, Helesys couldn't shake the oppressing feeling that the realm was not natural—not *right*. Helesys was one of the only people that would've been spared that fate, and on birthright alone. Yet she had volunteered to serve.

Memories came in flashes:

First was learning the ritual to create a simulacrum. Helesys was a young girl and stared back at a copy of herself. The spell created an exact copy, down to the pores on her skin and fibers of her clothes. The ritual itself wasn't hard, but maintaining concentration on it took every ounce of the young elf's strength. Even then, as a seasoned warrior, staring at the unblinking eyes of the copy was unsettling.

The next image was Helesys in Battle School. She was a young adult, not so much different in stature than she was now. The cadet stood next to a life-size stone statue of herself. It would act as a conduit for the simulacrum ritual, magnifying the power of the spell and reducing the strain on the caster. This time as Helesys cast the spell, dozens of copies of herself appeared all around the room. Their hair, skin, and clothes were gray with dull smatterings of the reds and purples that should've been there. It was as if the color had been drained away, or divided between them. But they moved! Each simulacra idly shifted their weight, touched their hair, or flexed their hands. The last thing Helesys heard was the praise of her teacher before the scene faded.

The grisly atmosphere of the shadowrealm returned—the horizon-spanning front of the Maw—and with it, Helesys in the silver armor of a commander. Elder Ianric stood beside her, overlooking the scene.

"We should push forward," Past Helesys said. "Between myself and Tyrisae, we could easily take the Gates of Ruins."

Elder Ianric shook her head. "You're young. To push forward is folly, and I will not risk the heir of House Byyra."

"I am here of my own free will—"

Ianric held up a hand to stay her. "I know, Helesys. You don't have to qualify yourself to me."

Past Helesys sighed. "It does no good. The elders will not listen."

"Need I remind you who is among their ranks?"

"No, Elder Ianric." Past Helesys licked her lips. "I... I resent heeding the decrees of those who have never fought on the front. They send the young to fight a war that they do not understand or even bear witness to—"

"That's enough, soldier."

Past Helesys nodded, and then stormed off, frustration muted on her face.

The scene changed again, this time to chaos. They stood on the steppes, overlooking the Passage of Sanhara. Helesys swelled with pride as the memory of the day came back to her. For decades, the simulacrum armies of the legion held the end of the passage as the shadowkind forces bottlenecked in the twisting passages below. Against orders, Helesys and her team had snuck across the steppes above, then bombarded the shadowkind forces before setting up their new fortifications in front of the passages and on the steppes above.

They were readying for the push to the Gates of Ruins, when Helesys's blood ran cold. *She remembered this day.*

From deep within the shadowkind's armies came a whirling mass of darkness—a siege beast from some ungodly realm beyond. The shadowkind dragged it across the sands and toward the steppes. It writhed like a sack of worms, like a black sun brought to the plane, spewing acidic darkness through the air.

Before Helesys could call for reinforcements, the sandy plain in front of them began to explode. Blastshells rained down from the legion's artillery—

Too close.

The sky in front of Helesys grew black with ash from the explosions and the cracks and cacophony of shells grew deafening.

The world went black.

~

Helesys was looking up at mountains and the bleeding sky, as she was hastily being carried away by soldiers. She felt cold, even in the thin air. Her vision went black, and all she heard were discordant voices and the whirring of clockwork equipment.

Helesys awoke to a blinding light, laying on a cold metal table. She was in a hospital room, surrounded by sterile metal. In spite of the numb haze, her body ached. Her right shoulder felt as if every nerve was on fire, and the pain was burning its way through her chest. She couldn't feel her feet—or her right arm. Helesys strained and lifted her head to see—she gasped at the sight.

In place of her right arm was an intricate gauntlet of mithral that shined a muted blue. It was a vicious-looking thing, with sharp lines and dagger-sharp fingers. Her shoulder—*Movernus help her.* She pulled back the sheet and found bright red wounds extending across her chest and stomach. It wasn't until she reached her shaking left hand up to touch them that she realized they were wires beneath her skin. Helesys blacked out a moment later.

~

More memories passed in a blur.

Aradi visited her in the hospital. Helesys couldn't bring herself to look at the sister, no matter how pleasant the surprise. The sterile walls were more of a comfort to look at than the conniving sister she has known for years.

Her mother didn't visit. Aradi made sure that Helesys knew that fact. This pained Helesys deeply.

Now the eldest daughter of House Byyra stood before the elders, wishing to return to the Eternal War. The elders listened patiently, but would not grant her wishes. Helesys was only vaguely aware that her mother was present and watching the hearing from the side of the room. She was groggy, and still in pain from her prosthetic arm. Helesys chose her words carefully—as carefully as a wounded animal could—but even in the hazy scene, she knew her words were full of vitriol and anger. The elders claimed that she is rash, impulsive, and her little tact is gone. They claimed that she is different—changed. Her mother's quiet sobs echo through the room. Helesys limped out of the council room, unable to walk without her mother's support.

Scenes flashed of Helesys in the hospital, relearning how to walk and how to write. Her metal arm was unruly, but there was a deep and desperate need to connect with it—to make it her own. Helesys knew she was stuck with it. The doctors told her that she was making progress—more than she had any right to. They wanted her to be thankful. She wasn't.

Time passed—how much, Helesys didn't know. She was sitting in a wing of House Byyra, a barren guest office. Something about it felt comfortable. Aradi walked in. Seized with sudden anger, Helesys grabbed her lying, conniving sister by the throat. Her metal arm gleamed in the light as she squeezed. Aradi smiled patiently. Aradi has a present for her, the location of something that Helesys wants—*Sala Gehenna*.

It is a mix of the old words. Almost gibberish. There are roots of suffering, salvation, and eternal life.

The scene changed. Her mother was in the barren office with her. Their faces are flush with emotion, but they stand the room apart.

Wynbella said, "You don't understand how bad the injury was. How close I came to losing you."

"You don't know either. I do!"

Her mother fell silent, fear writ large on her face.

Helesys's heart quaked. "I'm leaving. I'm leaving to find *Sala Gehenna*. I know where it is."

Wynbella's fear turns to disbelief. "*Sala Gehenna* doesn't exist. It's a tale told by deserters to frighten their children, to keep them from going into the forests at night." Her mother's words were timid, as if she didn't believe them.

~

The scene faded around Helesys, and gave way to a wide open field—a sea of dry, golden grass beneath a bleeding sunset.

A ghostly image appeared of Helesys and Taunauk stalking across the field, weapons drawn, as if they expected an attack to come at any moment. Meanwhile, the real heroes followed just behind the ghostly vision. The vision was eerily silent before them—the tense breathing of her and her comrades overshadowed it.

"This is before…" Helesys's voice was a choked whisper. She was afraid to speak any louder. "Before we were trapped…"

Her skin prickled—not at the vision of the distant past, but from the dread of whatever waited for them in that field.

In the fading twilight, the ghosts of Helesys and Taunauk stopped suddenly.

"*Where is Shawn?*" Past-Helesys said with barely contained fear. "*Where is he!*" she whispered.

The real Helesys's heart was beating in her throat, fear overtaking her. This was it—their last moments in reality.

The last moments before they saw *Sala Gehenna—the Dungeon.*

Before they were trapped.

"*Where is Shawn!*" Past-Helesys said, voice growing loud and feverish. Beside her, Past-Taunauk's teeth were bared in a panicked snarl.

Suddenly, the ghosts were gone, and the real heroes were alone, all three of them searching the golden field for danger. Helesys held close to her kindled power—the only solace she had.

And her eyes fell to the ground—to her own mutilated body. The body of Helesys lay twisted on the dirt. Her armor was shattered, tunic torn, her chest mangled. Her right arm gone, torn clean from the shoulder—bright red gushed from the wound, and pooled beneath her. She stared up at the sky, wide-eyed and utterly still.

The real Helesys stood over the grisly vision, afraid to breathe.

Blastshells echoed in the darkness.

Again, came the scenes of her being carried away by soldiers, the scene of her being laid on the operating table. But the ghost of Helesys lay unmoving—

Dead.

"I don't understand," Helesys muttered as she watched. Blastshells echoed in the sky like thunder.

Then came the quiet voice of her wand, *You died on that table, Helesys Byyra. It wasn't just your body that was decimated—your brain was damaged by the blastshell.*

But there was a chance to make you whole again. Just a chance.

In those dying moments, your higher brain functions were shutting down. You were nothing but pain, anguish, and raw emotion, without even the ability to scream.

The metal arm they fitted you with wasn't just a prosthetic. The wires joining us reach through your nerves, your spine, and your brain. They connected us so that together, you and I could rebuild your shattered mind.

Blastshells sounded in the sky like thunder.

Her wand said, *You asked me once how a wand could grow like I have, speak and think like I do. You have grown the same way. Grown and become something new, and together we have become a greater mage than any before us.*

You are a made-thing, Helesys Byyra.

And you have become so much more.

~

Helesys was silent, staring at the grisly image of her body on the operating table. She wasn't sure if Taunauk or Shawn were still beside her, or if they had seen any part of her memories.

She wasn't sure of anything anymore.

Helesys asked her wand quietly, *When did you know?*

I suspected your injuries were severe. This was confirmed when you saw yourself relearning how to walk and how to write. But I didn't know that you died. Not until now.

Helesys smirked to herself. *One-Mind repaired my gauntlet. It told me there was a connection that was severed before I was trapped here. I didn't hear your voice until after that… It was to keep us from speaking.*

That is my conclusion also.

But why?

A precaution. We are supposed to be one in the same. Two minds, working as one.

…So, are we separate? Are we still two minds?

No. We are linked, Helesys Byyra, and we always have been. Before you heard my voice, I was your intuition, your sense of magic and of danger. In an abstract way, you are talking to yourself.

Helesys smirked. *That seems a little too strange even for me. Besides, if we're one and the same…*

Helesys froze. She suddenly felt empty—as if something intangible had been stripped away from her. As if she had forever lost a dear memory.

Or perhaps, it was merely like a magician revealing the secret to their trick. Once known, the magic is gone forever.

Her voice barely a whisper, Helesys asked, *Wand, are you still with me?*

Silence answered.

~ ~ ~

Nonet

"Helesys, are you alright?" Shawn asked.

His voice was faint, and in the darkness, Helesys almost missed it.

"I'll be fine."

Her comrades came into view, appearing beside her. Taunauk placed a heavy hand on her shoulder. Deep shadows lined his face, making him look so much older than his years. Did the dungeon do that to them, or was it the recent revelations?

Helesys nodded to him and turned away. "Where are we?" she asked.

Slowly, the curtain of darkness receded, revealing an immense stone platform that stretched off into the black. The light seemed to come from above, but she could see no sun or candles anywhere. Behind them, one side of the platform stopped abruptly—this edge was lined with tiny parapet points. It reminded Helesys of the edge of a castle wall, or the edge of a stage. Helesys reminded herself that they were still in the realm of the paintings and that it was a strange realm.

The more Helesys dwelled on it, the more she felt that this was indeed a stage.

Opposite of the edge, light stretched out several hundred feet, slowly creeping until it revealed nine figures standing in a row—all Terran in form, save one: A giant whose metal skin glistened in the bright lights.

Even from a distance, Helesys recognized the red-haired channeler from before. She stood next to the same warrior and assassin that Taunauk and Shawn had fought earlier in the realm.

"You Chosen, say your thanks, for you walk upon hallowed ground," the channeler called, her voice carrying easily. "You walk a King's path."

Helesys sighed deeply and kindled power. Beside her, Taunauk and Shawn drew their weapons.

The channeler continued, "You fumble about blindly, barely able to grasp your own truth—let alone the magnitude of the task you undertake…"

Helesys tried to listen, but the revelations had drained her. She had no patience left for listening to monologues and no patience left for mercy.

"Are you done?" Helesys called, "or are you going to be in our way?"

For a moment, silence fell between them.

The Channeler said, "I suppose we *are* done. We are nine. We have been both less and more in times past. You have faced three of us, and shall now face the rest."

Four of the silhouetted figures stepped forward. Though they stood upright, they were clearly wolves—their white fur gleaming in the light. As they stepped into the light, they slunk to all fours and began to growl.

Three other figures stepped behind them—the channeler, the warrior, and the assassin. One by one, each Terran's skin split and they began to congeal with the wolves in front of them. When they were finished, each of the three wolves had turned a different color—the channeler's wolf blue; the assassin's black, the warrior's red—leaving the last wolf white.

The entire process was over in a blink—so fast it could hardly have been said to have happened at all. Helesys was only glad that she had not been close enough to see it in all of its grisly detail.

The wolves howled as one and charged across the stage. Only two figures remained behind—unmoving.

Helesys clutched the Gar of Shéslang and dredged power, bolstering herself and her gauntlet. She reached out and blasted. Arcane fury tore across the stage. The wolves dodged and weaved through the barrage. Errant blasts slammed into the wooden floor and blossomed into flares of purple.

Helesys cursed under her breath and readied her spear. Beside her, Taunauk smoldered with golden might, and Shawn's outline grew faint as he undid his arm wrappings.

The wolves were upon them a moment later. The white wolf seemed to glow as it lunged for Shawn, the rogue narrowly avoiding its first bite. Then the red wolf leapt for Taunauk and crashed into his shield with the force of an elephant, sending the glowing barbarian sliding back across the floor.

The blue wolf, its long hair shimmering with the colors of stormy water, circled around Helesys. A low growl sounded from its throat and Helesys felt the floorboards of the stage shift and rattle beneath her feet. It lunged a moment later. Helesys batted it away with her spear, but not before falling to her knees.

She reached out with her gauntlet for the lingering magic of the wolf's spell and canceled it with a holding spell.

The blue wolf snarled and crouched. Helesys was ready—

Something collided with her back, knocking the air from her lungs and sending her sprawling. She brought the spear up just in time to catch the mouth of the black wolf. Out of the corner of her eye, the blue wolf was nearly upon her.

"*Hieme Murum!*" Helesys shouted. The tendril of ice scraped against her nerves as it flicked out of her ring finger and surrounded her in a cocoon of ice. Muffled growls reached her.

Somewhere past the veil of white, Taunauk and Shawn's battles raged. Helesys only caught glimpses and blurs of gold.

The blue wolf leapt through the snowy shield, its fur flickering with searing blue flames. Helesys stepped to the side, fending off the beast with the spear. Even kept at bay, she could feel its fire magic. Soon the magic of the Ring of Winter would be spent.

So, Helesys channeled the rest of the ring's magic into a single spell, and compounded it with her spear—

"*Rigeh lancia!*"

The blue wolf leapt at Helesys. In an instant, the swirling vortex around the weaver coalesced, springing forth in a lance of solid ice. The spike pierced its chest—so thick it had nearly split the thing in two. The blue wolf twitched as it hung impaled.

Across the stage, Shawn and the white wolf were locked in a vicious ballet. Shawn's misty form slashed at the wolf as he danced just out of reach. The brilliant fur was now smattered with red blood.

"Helesys look out!" Taunauk cried.

The red wolf sprinted toward her. Helesys readied herself, but the beast barrelled past her. It leapt on its fallen blue comrade and tore into its flesh with a frenzy. It ate only for a moment before the act could no longer be called such—the red wolf's body cracked and twisted, pulling the dead wolf from the ice and assimilating it.

Helesys turned her gauntlet toward the creature and fired. Purple power smacked into the flank of the still half-formed thing, splattering gore across the planks of the stage.

But still the creature changed. Its fur grew dark purple. It turned and snarled, its mouth half-formed, bright red blood dripping from its fangs.

The abomination leapt toward Helesys, but Taunauk slammed into it with his shield, sending the two of them sprawling. A moment later, they stood—the Endroggen and the wolf faced each other down.

Helesys reached out with her magic, thinking that a holding spell and her ally's axe would make quick work of the creature. But as she uttered the words, she felt stabs of pain in her skull. Foul magic shielded the creature—the remnants of the blue wolf's magic. Helesys reeled from the psychic retaliation, vision swimming.

Taunauk and the purple wolf met each other in a clash of shield, axe, claw, and fang. For a moment, the two might've been a match. But slowly, golden warriors appeared by the barbarian's side, their weapons cleaving into the creature's flank.

Frenzied moments later, Helesys stood poised and found the battle already over. Taunauk and the golden warriors stood over the crippled body of the purple wolf.

Across the stage, Shawn and the white wolf slowed and began to circle each other. Both their chests heaved from exhaustion.

The white wolf lunged. Shawn flinched—the wolf sailed past him, catching the black wolf in its jaws. Its dark partner had been circling in the shadows, waiting for the time to strike. The white wolf bit down, and cracking bone echoed across the stage. The black wolf's chest began to rise, and for a moment, it seemed as if it had started breathing again. But the rasping, steady sound quickly became discordant.

The white wolf sprinted across the stage, dragging the body with it in powerful, loping strides. Even in that short sprint, its body began to twist and morph.

Taunauk and the glowing Endroggen were shoved aside as the creature slammed into its dying brethren—what had once been four wolves became a twisting, incoherent abomination. Its flesh was gray and seeping blood between its mangy patchwork of hair. Helesys's mind drifted back to the lumbering werewolf form that Matron Mildé had taken in the wode, walking on two legs and with a face somewhere between Terran and lupine, but it was a dream compared to the nightmare that stood in front of them. It lumbered toward Shawn. Each clawed hand that reached forward morphed into a mouth. Its body followed each new head, like flesh being poured down the sleeve of a shirt, moving in a pulsing discordant mass of skin and teeth.

Taunauk roared and leapt for the creature, axe cleaving through what should have been a neck. The severed head fell to the ground and rolled toward the twisting wolf—rejoining it. A new hand and then a head lunged for the barbarian. He was barely able to step out of the way.

With horrific speed, another mouth lunged for him—one of the golden warriors shoved the vessel aside. The wolf bit through both the golden warrior and its weapons, unperturbed. The glowing warrior vanished. Anguish and rage were writ large on his face.

Helesys had been about to turn her gauntlet on the abomination when she saw the other two enemies sprinting toward them. The ground trembled.

~

Shawn leapt into the fray, and together the wisp and the barbarian fought the twisted wolf creature.

Helesys considered the two quickly approaching foes—the shadow warrior and the metal giant. She knew the importance of numbers. They needed to focus their power and take down the wolf as quickly as possible. Numbers alone would give them the advantage.

Helesys called upon her fire magic. "*Immotalem immortalis.*" Fire leapt from her hand, growing and spreading through the air directly toward the writhing wolf. Taunauk and Shawn leapt back—

And the inferno faded a few feet from her hand. Embers fell to the ground. Helesys turned and found the shadow holding out a hand toward her—it reeked of magic. It had countered her fire spell.

The metal giant crossed the last twenty feet across the stage in a single step. It kicked at Taunauk and Shawn, sending the pair diving away and separating them from the wolf.

Helesys faced her dark counterpart. It stood nearly her height, and had the vaguest silhouette of armor and cowl, but there was no detail to its murky form. In its left hand, it held the curved shadow of a saber.

"I'll take the mage," Helesys called.

Taunauk growled, "The giant is mine."

"Good grief," Shawn muttered.

Helesys dredged power and turned toward the shadow mage. She raised her gauntlet and fired four arcane blasts, then ran toward the new foe. The shadow mage sidestepped and contorted its form to dodge the blasts, then raised its arm and fired four of its own.

The black beams of energy raced toward Helesys, and she funneled all power to her body, using the newfound strength to leap out of the way.

Then the sorceress and the mage were upon each other, colliding in a flash of spear and shadow. Each slash of her spear was blocked with a clang of the mage's saber. With each failed blow, Helesys called on more of her power and compounded it with the Gar of Shéslang—

And each time, the dark mage blocked her strikes. The fight became deafening, and the floorboards of the stage began to rattle beneath their feet. Helesys had used such power against monstrous creatures—and killed them—but the shadow mage was unfazed. Not once did it step backward. Not once did it lose its balance. It did not tire. It did not waiver.

Helesys screamed in frustration. Her arms trembled with each impact—her flesh and bones only surviving because of magic. The shadow stood between her and her allies, and Helesys could see the desperate battles beyond: Taunauk glowed golden, funneling all the strength of the spirits into himself, and was still forced to dodge the massive twin swords of the metal giant as they swung through the air; Meanwhile, Shawn's battle was shrouded in mist—only the ghoulish face of the wolf emerging as it searched for the rogue. Black wrappings blew across the stage and into the darkness.

Helesys needed this to be over quickly. The danger grew with each moment she was indisposed. If she couldn't beat the bastard in combat, she would break it with spells.

She slammed the butt of the spear to the floor. "*Terram crepitus!*" The floorboards cracked beneath the spear—

And the shadow slammed its own sword into the stage floor. "*Sile'.*"

The stage behind Helesys splintered. Shattered boards were hurled through the air, but the stage beneath the shadow—the stage toward the battles beyond—remained completely still.

Helesys stood aghast as floorboards rained down behind her. The shadow stared at her.

"*Restu sonmova, umbra,*" she said.

~

When Helesys used the holding spell, usually the world fell away, giving way to mindspace and the appearance of a misty realm. But that time, only her allies and enemies disappeared. Helesys and the shadow stood alone on the stage, surrounded by the same darkness.

"What are you?" she asked, trying to control her voice.

The shadow didn't answer.

A pit of fear took hold in Helesys's stomach.

"What are you?" she demanded.

The shadow didn't answer. It didn't move at all.

In the mindspace, Helesys lashed out with the Gar of Shéslang and the cursed shadow blocked every swing with its black saber.

The weaver stopped and stared. The spear trembled in her hands with rage and uncertainty. Beyond the darkness, she felt the tremors of her allies' battle.

Helesys grit her teeth and funneled as much power as she could into her gauntlet. The dark creature was nearly close enough to touch. A spreadblast couldn't miss.

Helesys raised her metal arm. Purple lightning crackled over the metal.

The shadow raised its right hand, mirroring her. Darkness churned around it.

Helesys fired. The shadow fired.

The world went white.

~

Helesys was thrown backward—tumbling across the stage.

When she finally stopped, her vision swam, and it felt as if her whole body pulsed with pain. She fought to stand.

Across the stage, Taunauk had separated into his glowing warriors. They swarmed the metal giant, cleaving into its joints. Despite their faces open in roars, Helesys couldn't hear anything over the ringing in her ears. Meanwhile, Shawn was slowing down. He was no longer mist incarnate, but blinks of dagger and flesh.

The shadow warrior stared back at Helesys—giving no indication that it had been phased by the explosion of their simultaneous attack.

Helesys swallowed dryly. Apprehension was building inside her. If she couldn't beat the shadow, perhaps she could aid her allies.

"*Restu sonmova*—"

"*Silentium.*"

The world fell quiet. Helesys could not hear anything—not the words of her spell, no roars or screams, or clash of swords. She only felt the quaking steps of the giant.

The shadow warrior stared at her expectantly.

If Helesys could not speak, then she couldn't cast most of her spells.

Instead, the weaver channeled her power to the simple blasts of her gauntlet. She raised a hand to fire at the metal giant, but the shadow warrior slashed at her arm. The blow did no real damage, but her blast flew errantly high.

Helesys fired again, this time tucking her arm close to her body. Again, the shadow slashed at her and Helesys was forced to twist out of the way. Her blast missed. Thrice more she tried, and each time the shadow harassed her, throwing off her shots.

Desperately, Helesys opened her mind to the magic, and found the spell of silence only affected a short area on the floor. If she could only get away from the damned shadow—

The creature harassed her at every step, lunging to stay in front of her—to keep her contained.

Helesys stopped, spear clenched in her hands. Her chest heaved, though she couldn't hear her own desperate breaths.

Across the stage, Taunauk, the spirits, and the giant still warred. But there was a crumpled heap where Shawn and the wolf had been. Helesys's heart pounded in her chest. What else could she do? She couldn't get past the shadow, couldn't help her comrades.

In a panic, she looked again to the heap where Shawn and the wolf had been and saw that it was little more than a mound of bloody fur.

Perhaps she didn't need to help them. Maybe Shawn had won on his own.

Helesys locked eyes with the shadow warrior. She stood still, and so did the creature. The entire time, it had merely been countering her—blocking her attacks, countering her magic, stopping her from getting to her allies. It hadn't attacked her, not outright.

The moment dragged on. Helesys didn't move. Neither did the shadow.

Meanwhile, the battle of metal and spirits raged on in silence. Helesys watched Taunauk and his spirits clamber and claw their way up the flank of the giant, only to be hurled down to the floor. Though every muscle and tendon in her body screamed at her to fight, Helesys did nothing—

The shadow's head toppled to the ground, then both the head and body vanished in a puff of black smoke. Shawn stood in front of her, a wisp of smoke trailing from his dagger. The black bandages were haphazardly wound around his forearms.

The rogue smiled. "Come on. Let's go help the big guy."

Helesys sighed and dredged power. Shawn took off toward the giant, and Helesys followed two steps behind. Free from the shadow's *silence* spell, the maelstrom of battle came alive again.

Shawn ran to the giant, then ran up its flank in a blur. The towering beast reached and pawed its shoulders. Horrid scrapes of metal echoed across the stage, but Shawn was much too fast.

Helesys stayed back from the fray, bolstering her gauntlet and firing at the giant's knee joints. Between her blasts and the Endroggen spirits assaulting it, the metal giant fell. Spirits leapt out of the way, and shards of floor were sent flying into the air. Together, the heroes descended upon the metal giant, cutting through its limbs and the chinks in its armor.

Taunauk struck last, severing its soulless head from its body. Then the bodies of the metal giant and the wolf abomination evaporated, turning to mist and floating off into the darkness.

~ ~ ~

To Walk a King's Path

The Endroggen spirits returned to their vessel. Then Helesys, Taunauk, and Shawn stood alone on the stage, surrounded by darkness. Their chests heaved from exertion. No trace remained of the nine.

"Damn," Shawn muttered. "We should've asked them how to get out of here." Taunauk chuckled and wiped the sweat from his brow.

Helesys said nothing as she stared off into the darkness. Instead, she turned her senses toward the seam. It lay out there—across the stage.

"Are you alright?" Shawn asked her. "You froze out there."

There was concern in his eyes, not accusation. Still, the truth was difficult to accept.

"I couldn't do anything," she said. "The shadow warrior countered my every move, even when I tried to aid you. But once I stopped fighting, it stopped too. It was a mirror, I think."

"This was no accident," Taunauk replied, stowing his axe in his backsling. "It was a test."

"What do you mean?" Shawn asked.

"We each had something to overcome."

Helesys added, "I had to trust you both. That's why I stopped fighting. I couldn't get past the shadow on my own. I trusted that one of you would defeat your opponent and come to my aid. That my allies would fight beside me."

Taunauk said, "Mine was similar. I could not best it with my strength and my rage, not even with the strength of my ancestors. I needed their golden spirits, and ultimately my comrades beside me."

"What about me?" Shawn asked. "What was my lesson? It wasn't about you guys helping me. I defeated the wolf on my own."

Taunauk said, "Maybe it is an omen that you will defeat the Wolf King, as the Voice said."

Shawn smiled faintly, trouble clearly written upon it. Then he pushed it aside, and his smile grew brighter. "I second that."

Helesys forced a smile. That was as good a theory as any other, but she had her own theory about the rogue's battle. She thought of the grandfather and the girl that had taken Shawn in and that he had ultimately left behind.

She said, "Perhaps your lesson was to show you that comrades are worth fighting for."

Shawn smirked, then laid a hand on her shoulder. "Good weaver, this is no time for feelings. Where's that seam?"

Both Helesys and Taunauk returned his mirth, and the weaver set to the task of finding the seam.

She led them into the darkness with her warding light. They found no other enemies, and some minutes later, they found the seam.

Helesys reached out for it, flaring her power. She felt the abyss of worlds open up before her. The worlds of the nine echoed in her head: Her and her allies *walk a King's path*. She

sensed there was meaning buried in the words, and so she held
the phrase in her mind as she sought their next world.
    There—Bone-white trees, heavy with fog.
    Together, the heroes stepped through the seam.

~ ~ ~

NEXT TIME ON
*A BATTLEAXE AND
A METAL ARM*
Book 16:

The Slumbering Bog
Available July 2022

Spoiler–Free excerpt from *BAMA 16*

Soon, the ground beneath their feet grew damp, and then laden with water. Step by step they sank deeper into the swamp, the muck squelching beneath their boots, each step releasing a sour, earthen smell. For as unpleasant as the swamp looked, Helesys found it strange that they hadn't smelled much of anything until that point—only when the muck beneath their feet was disturbed.

A memory of a spell came to her, unbidden. "*Aqua deambulatio,*" she said. Slowly, the three heroes rose higher in the swamp until they were standing on top of the twisted grasses. Both Taunauk and Shawn paused to watch their feet.

Shawn said, "Your spell recall is fabulous, really. But you couldn't have remembered that *before* my boots got wet?"

"Of course not," she said jokingly. "Besides, I can't just remember all the spells I used to know. It seems like I need *something* to trigger my memory."

"I'm only half serious," the rogue added. "I appreciate you. So, how do you know so many spells? I admit, I don't remember a lot of mages, but you know a lot, and you know spells from different schools of magic."

Helesys thought back on her revelation. She was an accomplished mage, but she was also a made-thing, directly connected to her wand. She had years of knowledge and the innate magical abilities from the wand itself—something she still didn't fully understand.

In their time through the dungeon, Helesys, Taunauk, and Shawn had shared nearly everything with each other: All of their recaptured memories and all of their struggles. But Helesys felt uneasy at the thought of telling her companions that she had died on the battlefield, that she'd been brought back from death, and turned into something else.

To be continued July 2022

Thank you for Reading

I hope you enjoyed reading this story as much as I enjoyed writing it.

If you did, I would massively appreciate a short review on Amazon or your favorite book website. Reviews are crucial for any author, and a starred review or even just a line or two can make a huge difference.

It's especially true for the start of a series. Thanks and I hope you enjoy the next one!

Looking for more Engrossing Fantasy?

You might like **Tales from Another World,** an ongoing short story series containing stories about sorcerers, druids, mortals, gods, thieves, and all other manner of Terrans.

The 2nd and 3rd installments are out and they tie into the outside world of *A Battleaxe and a Metal Arm.* So, if you're looking for more engrossing fantasy stories, and if you want to know more about this fantasy universe, read on and see how deep the rabbit hole goes.

What questions do you have about *A Battleaxe and a Metal Arm*?

If you've read this far, hopefully you'll read a bit further—both in this book and across the series. I'm not sure how most authors write serials and how much of it is flying by the seat of their pants, but that's not how I do things. For all the major questions that might come up in BAMA, I already have answers for 95% of them. Same goes for the major plot points, twists and climaxes. That might sound boring to some, especially some of you other authors who enjoy variations of writing into the dark, but I think having a solid blueprint is paramount to writing a long series.

So, what questions do you have about the story? Here are a few:

1) ~~What is the dungeon?~~ It's a soul trap of overwhelming size and power. But where did it come from? Is it a force of nature or an ill-made weapon, or perhaps something else entirely? In the real world, it looks like a giant cloud with faces writhing just beneath the surface. Helesys speculates that the

reason no one remembers it is because it's so horrific their minds blot it out!

2) ~~Who was Helesys before she got trapped~~? We've learned that Helesys was both a soldier and was the oldest daughter of the elven Great House Byyra.

3) ~~Who was Taunauk before he got trapped~~? There was an omen of a blight in the Endroggen heaven, Accaelum. Taunauk is an Endroggen barbarian who was raised as a warrior and a vessel. His purpose was to one day free the trapped Endroggen souls from the Dungeon.

4) How well did they know each other beforehand?

5) How did Helesys get her metal arm? Likely through injury, amputation, and replacement. She was likely fighting in the Eternal War, the war of the Elves against the Shadowkind.

6) ~~Who is Shawn~~? He is a wisp from the plane of dreams. One who walks through the dreams of elves and humans, while being neither. He has lived as both a god and a mortal. His kind is on the run from the elder god, Nimicus.

7) Why does Shawn feel so familiar to Helesys and Taunauk? The group speculates that they were traveling together for unknown reasons. Shawn worries that they were tracking him. This could explain why Helesys and Taunauk are always reborn together, while Shawn was usually alone.

7) Who is the Wolf King and what sinister plans does he have for our heroes? How did he come to rule over the Dungeon? How does the Gatekeeper factor into all this?

8) Who is the mysterious voice encountered on the white sandy shores of Meridian? Why do they seek the death of the Wolf-King? ...And why did they choose the heroes? The Voice might be the Gatekeeper... but the truth is still unknown...

Did I miss any questions? Probably. Connect with me and other *BAMA* fans on social media and compare questions!

I've got plans. I've got answers. And I've got them on a drip-feed. Keep reading and expect to find out a little more to the mysteries with each installment. Hopefully, you're as excited about this series as I am.

Connect with the Author

If you want to stay up to date on the latest about Samuel's publishing news and blog, check out his website and consider signing up for his monthly newsletter.

www.SamuelFlemingBooks.com

Samuel can also be found on Reddit, Tiktok, and Facebook.

Samuel Fleming is a Science Fiction and Fantasy author.

He grew up in Maryland, spending most of his time swimming and writing. Swimming gave him a lot of time to daydream, so the two hobbies complemented each other well. Idle day dreams turned into stories, some of which stuck with him for years. These days he swims a little less and writes a lot more.

He loves a good story no matter the medium: Books, TV, video games, comics, tabletop RPG's, or podcasts—most of which he attempts to share with his wife and three kids, and occasionally on his blog.